The runaway alien

Karen Inglis

Cover illustration by Karen Inglis and Damir Kundalić
Interior illustrations by Damir Kundalić

www.eeekthealien.com

~WS~
Well Said Press

Published by Well Said Press 2012
83 Castelnau, London, SW13 9RT, England

ISBN: 978-0-9569323-3-4

www.wellsaidpress.com

For Bob, George and Nick - better late than never!

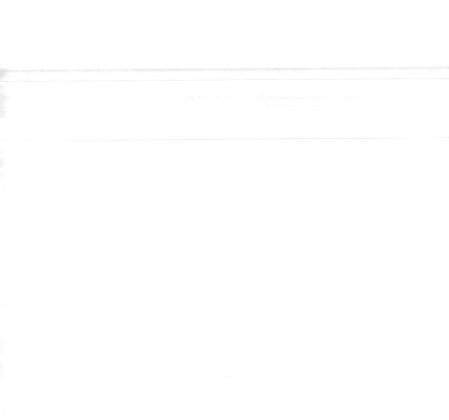

One

It was a fairly typical Saturday morning in our house. Dad was in the garden emptying out the shed (again!). Mum had gone to the gym for her early morning workout. Rory (my four-year-old brother) was on the sofa wearing Dad's snorkel and mask watching his favourite underwater scene in 'Finding Nemo'. I was scoring goals against the kitchen wall in front of an imaginary crowd of 50,000.

That's when the doorbell rang.

'I'll get it!' I shouted. I don't know why I shouted, because I knew that neither Dad nor Rory could hear me. As I rushed down the hall to open the front door I tried to guess which of the following it would be:

- Little Joe Williams from next door asking for his football back (yet again!)
- Someone selling tea towels

- Our postman with a parcel
- The National Lottery man to say we'd won (dream on!)

or

- Mum, hot and sweaty after the gym, having forgotten her key as usual

In fact it was none of these. Standing at our door that Saturday morning was, I'm not kidding you, an *alien!*

Now, most people would jump out of their skins at the sight on their doorstep of a bald-headed fluorescent green monster with pale blue smoke wafting from its tiny semicircular ears. But there was something about this alien that touched my heart. Whether it was his large slow-blinking pink-red eyes, his snub nose, his friendly smile, or simply the fact that he was exactly my height, I cannot tell you, but for some reason I just stood there and gawped at him in wonder.

My gawping, and the alien's blinking and smiling, carried on for a good thirty seconds. It was as if I had met a long lost friend and here we were bonding again. But then I nearly jumped out of my skin as an eerie wheezing and rasping noise floated up from behind my right shoulder.

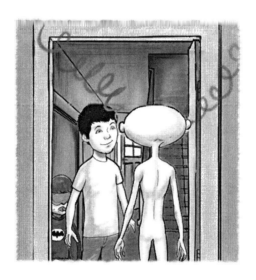

The alien suddenly stopped blinking and pulled such a terrified face as he stared beyond me I was convinced that an enemy being from the far side of Mercury must have zapped down into my house to do battle with him. I swung round in fear for my life - to find Rory, complete with snorkel and mask, staring wide-eyed through his steamed-up visor at our visitor.

The alien couldn't handle the sight of Rory. I think it was the batman outfit that finished him off. Without warning he emitted a strange high-pitched echoing sound, then turned and fled out through our gate and off down the road.

'You idiot, Rory!' I shouted. Rory wheezed through his snorkel, then shrugged his shoulders and hold up both hands as if to say, 'What did I do?' Then he disappeared back to his 'Finding Nemo' DVD, whisking his cape behind him like a matador with attitude.

'Well,' I thought to myself, 'I've got two choices here. Either I close the door and pretend this never happened, *or* I race down the road to see if I can find the alien and bring him back.' No prizes for guessing which of these two options I picked.

By the time I got to the gate my fluorescent green friend had almost reached the end of our road.

'Come back!' I called in a feeble voice, knowing he wouldn't hear me.

Just at that moment an almighty roar filled the morning sky. I looked up to see the Red Arrows streak out through the white-grey clouds, and cut a cool formation right over the top of the houses at the end of the road. Awesome! When I glanced to the end of the road again, the alien had stopped and was jumping up and down in a frenzy, pointing at the planes.

'Poor soul!' I said to myself. 'Probably thinks it's

his spaceship come to rescue him.' It would take more than a puff of blue ear-smoke to get him a ride on one of those! And they definitely wouldn't be taking him home – to the government laboratories more likely!

As their last echo faded across the sky the alien, who had calmed down, didn't, as I thought he would, shoot off around the corner. Instead he stood there gazing dreamily into the sky, as if he'd just seen Father Christmas and his reindeers, or a few stray angels.

'An alien trance!' I thought as I started walking towards him. At that moment (had he heard my thoughts?) he switched his gaze out of the sky and down the road towards me. Immediately he started waving vigorously. As I approached I could see a broad grin on his moon-shaped face. He seemed to have found his long-lost soul mate again.

'That was the Red Arrows!' I declared with a smile. The alien nodded enthusiastically. 'Did you think they might be your spaceship?' He took a step back a pace and frowned indignantly, as if I'd just said something really dumb. 'So, you speak English?' I faltered, glimpsing his flat, long-toed feet. He pulled a stiff upside-down smile, then gestured as if adjusting an invisible shower control. By this, I think he meant, 'A little.'

'Where do you come from?' I asked, my eyes following his trails of blue smoke upwards.

'**Eeek!**' screeched the alien in a strange echo, pointing to the sky.

'Of course!' I said smiling. 'I know all about the planets - got a poster in my room, and lots of books. D'you want to come and see? You could show me your home!' I could barely believe my luck when the alien shrugged his shoulders and smiled shyly, as if to say, 'Why not?'

Two

Dad was still in the shed and, judging by the thumps I could hear through the living room wall, Rory was practising diving into the ocean from the sofa. (Either that, or – another of his favourite games – playing Batman leaping from the Empire State Building to catch a baddy.) Mum was still out.

With the coast clear, and, as you might imagine, more than a little excited, I took my alien friend straight up the stairs to my bedroom.

As I opened the door my enormous map of the universe confronted us, hanging directly above my bed, on the opposite side of the room.

I realised at this point it was probably my interest in space (so often mocked by others) that had singled me out for this special visit from an extraterrestrial being. Suddenly I felt privileged. Proud beyond words. Thinking of what my friends were probably doing at this precise moment, I also felt extremely smug.

'Here it is!' I cried confidently, scrambling onto my bed and diving towards the map. 'Now, where are you from?'

No 'Eeek' in reply. No already familiar pant of cool breath behind me. I looked around. To my horror the alien had vanished! Only thin air hovered in my doorway.

'Friend...where are you?' My heart beat furiously. Could I have imagined all this? Just then, to my delight, a puff of blue smoke rose from the foot of my bed, whereupon the alien stood up grinning from ear to ear - holding out my football boots!

'How do you do that?' I gasped, staring at the edges of his mouth. (I swear they *really were* touching his ears!) But my friend wasn't listening. Instead he was fiddling with the laces of the boots, echoing a low hum. Still ignoring me, he sat down on my bed and started putting my boots on. I, meanwhile, began eagerly pointing at my map of the universe quoting the names of the planets, which had moons and how many, and trying to guess which outreach my friend might have come from.

My boots seemed to fit him perfectly, though did look pretty stupid on the end of a pair of knobbly kneed, spindly fluorescent green legs!

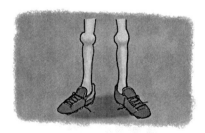

'Eeek', as I decided to call him, was now wandering around my room showing more interest in my football posters than any of my space stuff. He even tossed my Stargazer telescope aside in favour of my Northbridge United scarf, which he slung around his neck as he continued to rifle through the mess on my desk. Finally I gave up my tour of the universe and scrambled off my bed. Eeek by now was sitting on the floor thumbing through the pages of my World Cup Sticker Book.

When he reached the England team he suddenly stopped and his pale pink eyes filled with tears. Then a pear-shaped drop of water rolled down over his glowing green cheek and landed 'Splat!' right on Joe Carraber's head.

'Hey! Be careful with that!' I lunged forward. Immediately I regretted my outburst, for as I now clutched the book to my chest I could see more and more tears welling in my friend's eyes and, within moments, Eeek was rolling around on the carpet in a near puddle of water, sobbing with a strange echo.

'Look, Eeek, what is it?' I said with a sigh. This alien thing wasn't turning out to be half the fun I'd hoped. Let's face it, what self-respecting 11-year-old wants to spend their Saturday morning with a *crying* alien?

Eeek slowly gathered himself together and wiped away his remaining tears. He then gestured for the book, which I handed over - not without trepidation.

Eeek placed the book on the carpet and eagerly pointed at the sticker of Northbridge United and England striker, Steve Mitchell.

'Steve Mitchell!' I said with a smile. Eeek nodded

enthusiastically. 'Great player!' I added. Eeek clapped his hands. Now we were getting somewhere. 'Hang on? You *know* about Steve Mitchell?' I was talking to *an alien* after all!

Eeek confronted me with another of his indignant frowns.

'Nasty ankle injury,' I muttered vacantly. 'I hope he's okay for England-Brazil on Friday!'

To my horror, Eeek's eyes immediately began glistening again. 'Oh no, Eeek, please! No more crying!' I now had my sanity to think of - not to mention my sodden carpet.

I was glad of my outburst, despite his tears, because Eeek suddenly pulled himself together, jumped up and started practising air kicks in front of my mirror.

'So!' I said. 'You know about the World Cup and the EnglandFootball Team! What else do you know about?'

Eeek gave a knowing wink, then climbed onto the middle of my bed and crossed his spindly legs. A glazed look came over his eyes as he now pointed at his tummy and started rubbing it as he hummed in a high pitch. 'Oh dear, you're hungry!' I said,

11

now wondering what aliens ate for lunch.

Eeek shook his head impatiently then pointed to his tummy again as if to say, 'Look!'

I stared hard at the spot where his belly button should have been, but wasn't. Next thing a rectangle began drawing itself into his translucent green skin. I gasped in horror. '*Oh my God! You're a Telotubbic, aren't you? I'm on "You've Been Framed!" aren't I?*' How would I ever live this one down!

Eeek instantly raised his pale pink eyes to the ceiling, then tossed me a cool glance as if to say, 'Boy you really *are* dumb!' He then pointed impatiently at the rectangle in his tummy, which by now was opening like a sideways cat flap.

As the door into Eeek's tummy opened wider, so too did my mouth. By the time Eeek started reaching *inside* his tummy, I swear, my bottom jaw was all but on the duvet where I sat opposite him.

'What on *earth* are you doing?' I shrieked, fully expecting a blood-soaked intestine to flop out at any moment. (My mum's face on seeing a blood-soaked duvet, along with me and an alien on it, wasn't far from my mind either.)

Eeek echoed a chuckle, and carried on smiling and shaking his head knowingly as his frail green arm reached deeper and deeper inside his tummy. I was now waiting for his hand to appear out the other side of his back, like a scene from a late night horror film, but it somehow didn't.

'Eeeeeek!' he finally squealed, as though he'd found what he'd been looking for. My friendly green alien then yanked his hand out and dropped a small purple glowing case onto my bed. It looked a bit like a little lunch box. The small door in his tummy conveniently closed itself and disappeared.

Three

For a few moments we both sat staring at the case expectantly, like there was a bomb in it or something. Then, as Eeek slowly reached forward, I jumped up to close my bedroom door. Who only knew what might come crawling, flying or beaming out of an alien's luggage!

Eeek certainly moved quickly, for by the time I turned around he was already spreading out the contents of the case onto my bed. They included:

- a miniature globe of the Earth
- a photo of *me* watching television!
- a set of miniature Red Arrows planes
- an England Football Supporters' membership card
- what looked like an airline ticket
- a poster of Steve Mitchell (folded)

- a small rectangular screen - a bit like an iPad or mini TV

and

- a framed photograph of a group of aliens!

'*Wow!* Is that your family?' I pounced on the group photograph. Eeek nodded proudly. 'Your mum and dad?' (I couldn't tell one from the other). Eeek nodded. 'You?' Eager nod. 'Little sister?' (Now pointing at the smallest alien.) Vigorous headshake and puff of blue smoke. 'Little brother?' Ear-touching alien grin.

'Eeek...why have you come here?' I asked casually. Eeek shook his head uncooperatively.

'Okay, so how did you get this England Supporters' card? *And* a photo of *me?*' Poor Eeek didn't get a chance to answer, because suddenly it was my turn to act indignant. 'Have you been *spying* on me?' I asked warily. Eeek nodded enthusiastically, which only made me frown all the more. Then he picked up the little screen, which immediately began to illuminate.

Gulping down my pride I shuffled up for a closer look. Eeek's breath was cold on my knee. As his arm brushed against me it felt cool and hard, like a snake's. But I didn't mind.

The screen showed an image of what looked like a bedroom or study. Eeek pointed proudly at his chest, then back at the screen where I suddenly saw him, Eeek, sitting side-view at a desk to the left, poring over a book and with a laptop to one side.

The room had a map of the world on the wall behind Eeek's desk, an inflatable globe of the Earth hanging from the ceiling and a poster of the Red Arrows on the far wall, to the right of the door. Underneath the Red Arrows poster was a large picture of the World Cup itself. All very cool!

Eeek tapped the screen, to make sure I was concentrating. Suddenly the Eeek I could see inside the screen got up and pointed a fluorescent finger at the empty wall opposite his desk. Instantly a giant screen appeared from nowhere and illuminated with – hey! – last Wednesday's England v Cameroon match just kicking off! The Eeek inside the television sat back down with a grin, crossed his arms and legs and started watching.

'Cool! *That's* your bedroom!' I cried in delight, my eyes still following the match. But suddenly his bedroom door opened. The silhouette of an adult alien filled the doorway and Eeek jumped up from his chair.

'That your mum?' I whispered nervously. Eeek nodded dolefully. Judging by the scowl on her face and the dense jets of blue smoke spurting from her ears Eeek's mum wasn't best pleased.

It took Eeek's alien mum precisely one piercing glance to disappear the football match from the wall. Now I was upset - we were about to miss a goal! The image on Eeek's wall was replaced with a bare room in which an adult alien was scribbling signs on a whiteboard while green and pink smoke billowed from a test tube.

Eeek's mother frogmarched my alien friend back to his chair, threw her arms into the air, and marched out.

'Wow, Eeek, you've been bunking off your lessons!' I cried.

Eeek nodded and gave me a big grin.

Back on the little television Eeek, who now had a defiant look on his face, was standing up from his chair again. Slowly he raised one arm and pointed his glowing forefinger at the screen on the wall. The image of the alien teacher dissolved and was immediately replaced by - *my house!* Eeek thrust his finger angrily at the wall once more. This time it was me who appeared! Me, at home, *watching the same football match on telly!*

With his eye still half on the big screen, Eeek reached under his desk and yanked out the same fluorescent purple case he had with him now. He laid it on his desk amongst his papers, flipped the lid open and marched across to a small chest of drawers and began taking things out. He then picked up his family photograph and, on returning to his desk, began furiously throwing everything into the case.

I quickly realised these were the very things which now lay around us on the bed. Eeek closed his case, then began furiously tapping a message on his laptop.

'Eeek!' I said with a gasp, looking up. 'You've run away from home!'

Eeek took in a deep breath, delivered an ear-touching grin, then sent defiant puffs of deep blue smoke wafting into the air.

As for me, I was dumbstruck! This alien had run away to Earth - and he'd run away to be with *me!*

Four

Now I knew Eeek was a runaway alien, many things became clear. His bedroom covered with Earth stuff. His excitement at the sight of the Red Arrows. His obsession with the England Football Team.

Eeek must have dreamed of going to Earth just as I had so often dreamed of travelling into space. The only difference, of course, was Eeek could actually do it.

But how long had my alien come to stay for? And why had he chosen me?

These were questions that needed answers.

Thump...thump...thump! A grown-up was climbing the stairs. I stared at Eeek in horror. He was about to be discovered by *my dad!* The door handle rattled. The door flung open. It was Rory - snorkel, batman suit and all - wheezing right at me again. I say 'me' because Eeek, miraculously, wasn't there any more. Nor were any of his belongings.

Rory wrenched the snorkel tube from his mouth. 'Where's that alien?' he demanded, squinting right at me through his mask. It was then that I noticed his flippers.

'What alien, dummy?' I replied. Rory didn't answer. He just shoved his snorkel tube back in, glanced around the room like a wary frogman, then thumped out. 'Mind the stairs in those flippers!' I shouted. Too late.

Rory's wailing at the foot of the stairs finally subsided, and the living room door slammed shut.

'Eeek! Where are you?' I whispered. No reply. I now spent several minutes looking for him.

Under my bed? No. In the wardrobe? No. Outside

on the window ledge? No. In my dirty underwear basket? Phew, no!

My heart sank. No alien. No 'Eeek'. Not a wisp of blue smoke, nor the hint of an echo. I flung myself back on my bed in despair - only to come face to face with Eeek, splayed across my ceiling like a grinning green gingerbread man.

I had barely begun to enjoy my relief when, 'rat, tat, tat!', someone was knocking at the front door.

'That must be Mum,' I said. 'Forgotten her keys again.' Dad was still in the shed. Rory had the TV on full volume. 'Don't go away!' I whispered up. Then rushed down.

In fact it wasn't Mum. It was an eager young man selling tea towels.

Luckily Mum appeared at the gate right behind him just as I opened the door. She immediately told him that she had enough tea towels to start up a tea-towel rental company. The eager young man disappeared with a scowl. Mum switched off her iPod and jogged in.

'Had a good morning dear?' she panted as she passed.

'Out of this world!' I said with a snigger.

'Great!' she called, heading into the garden for a stretch.

The lawn was scattered with garden tools, boxes of nails and screws, an old lawn mower and several identical packets of plant fertiliser. Dad poked his head out of the shed and smiled. He was in heaven! Mum started stretching between a fallen rake and the rusty barbecue.

Unfortunately, as I turned to head back to my room Rory appeared. He had removed his flippers and breathing tube, and had his snorkel mask pushed up on top of his head.

'Mum! We had an alien at the door this morning!' he shouted eagerly.

'Did you, dear?' Mum was smiling sideways, her left ear almost touching the lawn as she stretched.

'No, I mean a real one! Charlie spoke to it, didn't you Charlie?'

'Yes, Rory,' I said with a smile. I rolled my eyes at Mum. She raised her eyebrows, smiled back then winked.

'Right, I'm going to do my homework,' I said, trying not to smirk.

Rory stood frowning at the lawn as I hurried past.

Five

When I got back upstairs I found Eeek happy in my room   *tidying up!*

'Eeek, what are you doing?' I gasped. Ear-to-ear alien grin. I had never seen my desk so organised, my rubbish bin so full, the books on my bookshelf so upright, nor my 187 Premier League swap stickers so neatly piled. Eeek beamed at me proudly. This was one tidy alien.

'My, you *have* done a super job!' Mum, who must have followed me up, was looming in the doorway. Typical. She has this ability to appear just when you don't want her to. Like the time I was just *talking* about smoking with my best friend Jake. I'm sure she has a sixth sense.

In a panic I looked around. To my relief Eeek had disappeared again - presumably onto the ceiling. 'Hi!' I squeaked in a guilty pitch. I fixed a stare on the carpet to stop myself looking up.

'Must get this room repainted!' Mum muttered,

glancing at the ceiling.

I immediately felt the blood drain from my cheeks, but then, to my relief, spotted blue smoke rings rising from behind my wardrobe - not to mention a few alien limbs poking out.

'Yes, well...' I said with a stiff smile, starting to close my door on her, 'must get on...want to finish my homework. I'm having tea at Jake's, remember.'

Jake Chester's my best friend. He lives four doors down from me, which is great because I can go there without being escorted like a child. Eeek agreed to stay in my room and hide if anyone came in. He also indicated he didn't mind if I told Jake about him. Very accommodating this alien friend of mine!

'An alien! Ha ha! Very funny!' snorted Jake. Jake doesn't like to be made a fool of.

Nor, for that matter, do I.

'I'm serious!' I said. 'He's run away from space! Blue ear-smoke. Cat-flap tummy. Magic finger - I swear!'

'Oh yeah,' sneered Jake, 'and did I tell you about those goblins at the bottom of my garden?' My best friend was getting irritated. We should have been outside playing cricket.

'Okay! Come and meet him!' I challenged. Jake frowned, but how could he refuse?

Jake and I stormed up my stairs and burst into my room. It was then that I realised Eeek had a sixth sense even better than my mum's, because he had made no attempt to hide himself. Instead we found him sitting comfortably on my bed with his little television screen propped against his knees and my Northbridge United scarf still wrapped around his neck. My football boots were on the floor.

'What *are* you looking at, Eeek?' I asked, suddenly forgetting about Jake.

'*Eeek!*' said my friend with a smile. I climbed onto the bed next to him and looked into the screen which was flashing up the latest football results. Holland had just beaten Chile 3-2.

'You're more into football than I am!' I said laughing.

It was at this point Jake slumped to the floor.

'**EEEEeek!**' shrieked my friend. We dived to the ground and lifted Jake onto my bed. As we did so our eyes met and I felt Eeek's cold breath on my cheek. It didn't bother me - or spook me - I swear. It just felt special. Like I had a blood brother or twin. Jake groaned as he began to come round. Eeek thoughtfully stepped back two paces.

'Whoa! Cool!' gasped Jake, sitting up, eyes saucer-like. Eeek was flashing one of his ear-to-ear grins while blue smoke billowed from his ears. For a minute I thought he was flirting with my best friend!

Jake's pretty reliable. That's why he's my best friend. It turned out I had judged things right and we were soon all three getting on like a house on fire. Eeek let us watch the football results on his little TV screen. He then showed us a few alien tricks - like making one of his Red Arrow planes fly around the room (awesome!) and getting objects to disappear only to reappear somewhere else. Next thing he had picked up his globe and was staring hard at that. The harder he stared, the faster it began to spin. Suddenly I felt dizzy, and spotted Jake trying to keep his balance.

'Stop!' I yelled. Luckily Eeek did.

'Charlie! Are you all right in there?' My mum burst through the door with a towel wrapped round her head like a turban. Eeek, needless to say, had vanished. 'I think we've just had a tremor!' she exclaimed.

'A tremor?' I looked blank.

'An *earth* tremor, dear. I'd better ring the police, just in case. No, on second thoughts the council.' Mum shut the door. 'Anyway, I thought you were at Jake's!' she shouted thundering down the stairs. Despite all the time she spends trying to get fit, Mum really can sound like a herd of buffalo.

That night the evening news was full of reports about the local earth tremor. 'Measured 3.5 on the

Richter Scale,' said the newscaster. 'Never known anything like it in these parts.'

Eeek promised never to do it again.

Six

Sunday morning was football club. Our team (Rockstone Lane!) was due to play our biggest rivals (the Southdown Eagles). Eeek had spent the night on my ceiling. Don't ask. I'm not an alien. I decided I would find out more about his plans after I got back from the match.

When I started putting on my football gear Eeek got all excited and started diving for imaginary goals across my carpet.

'Steady on, Eeek!' I said with a chuckle. 'You'll wake the house.' He ignored me. 'Right, I'm off to play football,' I said with a smile. 'I'll be back at lunchtime.'

Eeek suddenly jumped to attention, started batting his eyelids and gave me a broad grin. Then he pointed at his chest and nodded.

'No way!' I blurted out, stepping back in surprise. 'No way! You'll be seen!'

Instantly, pale pink tears began welling in Eeek's

eyes. Now I felt a right idiot and more than a little guilty. How could I have been so thoughtless? 'No, please don't cry, Eeek,' I pleaded. 'I just want to protect you.' It was then that the door opened and Jake walked in.

'Morning!' he whispered excitedly, closing the door behind him 'How's it going?' He raised his eyebrows at me then smiled sweetly at my alien friend. This, for some reason, annoyed me.

'Eeek wants to come to football,' I said nervously.

'Great idea! You can be our team mascot!' said Jake beaming.

'Jake, don't be stupid!' I spluttered. I could already feel myself trembling.

'Oh, it'll be fine!' he said confidently. 'Gus Whiting's brother turned up in a gorilla outfit a few weeks ago. No-one even batted an eyelid!'

Eeek, as you might imagine, was looking more and more pleased as Jake rattled on. I wasn't convinced, but in the end it was two against one.

'See you later!' I called to my parents, who were reading the papers in bed.

As we crept down the stairs Rory - up early as usual - emerged from the kitchen with a dry Wheetabix in his hand. I swear Rory gets up at 4am every day - I reckon that's why he's so hyper half the time.

'Hide Eeek!' I quickly whispered to Jake behind

me. No need. Eeek had already disappeared.

It was Jake's dad's turn to take us to football and I nervously held my breath as we climbed into the car. Where had my fluorescent friend gone? Would he suddenly appear from under a seat? Had he hidden in the boot? The glove compartment? Oh blimey - the engine!

Jake shot me a puzzled frown as his father drove off. I shrugged my shoulders and looked at the road ahead.

The car ride to our football ground takes about fifteen minutes. After about five I had a brainwave.

'I wonder if Myles Mackinlay will turn up as an alien!' I said, then nudged Jake hard in the ribs.

Jake gave a knowing smile.

'An alien mascot? Whatever next!' chortled Mr Chester. I sometimes wonder if I'm too smart for my own good.

As we climbed out of the car Eeek emerged from behind a tree.

He was wearing a pair of my tracksuit bottoms, my black trainers and my red and white Northbridge United scarf. A smart move, though he could have done with a T-shirt.

'Here's Myles the alien!' bellowed Jake. Eeek walked slowly towards us, blue smoke wafting from his ears. Mr Chester pushed his glasses down his nose and peered over. 'My goodness - now that is some outfit!' Eeek nodded and smiled.

'He never talks when he's doing his alien thing,' I said. 'Takes his part very seriously. Wants to be an actor, you know.'

Mr Chester's stare soon metamorphosed into a frown. He clearly wasn't altogether sure of what to make of Eeek but wasn't about to let on. He cleared his throat and shook his head.

'Er...right, let's get over there, shall we boys?'

I mean, he was hardly going to say, 'That's no actor, that's a *real* alien,' was he now?

Jake's dad found himself a chair and hid behind his newspaper. He's not really interested in football. Not like my dad who prances up and down on the sideline shouting words of 'encouragement', which is just annoying and embarrassing.

Out of earshot of Jake's dad we introduced Eeek as my second cousin, Myles, a child actor from a science fiction programme about life on Mars.

Our story got a little confusing, because we hadn't planned it. It sort of grew out of the actor thing I had said to Jake's dad. Still, as Jake predicted, everyone was so busy getting on their boots and talking about last night's earth tremor, they barely batted an eyelid.

'Great costume!' someone managed. But that was all.

Most of the parents who stayed to watch kept a safe distance from Eeek. They obviously thought he was 'odd'. Eeek was quite happy with this. He spent the whole time running up and down the far side of the pitch, in line with the ball.

When the other side scored he stood with his arms folded and fierce blue smoke billowing from his ears. 'Turn it down will you!' I muttered running past. The billows turned to pale wisps, barely visible across the pitch. I winked, and Eeek smiled back.

It was about midway through the second half that something dramatic happened. I suppose I should have known better than to expect the morning to pass completely smoothly. Cameron Hicks, who'd been stuck in a massive traffic jam, arrived late. Cameron (AKA 'Hicksy') is an ace soccer player, and our key striker. Thinking about it, I suppose he does resemble England striker Steve Mitchell.

Anyway, so Cameron swans onto the pitch as a late substitute. At this point it was 1-0 to them. Two minutes after his substitution he scored an ace shot into the top right-hand corner of the net. We went crazy. So, unfortunately, did Eeek.

There we all were slapping Cameron heartily on the back and putting our arms around his neck, just like they do on the telly. The next thing, we hear a high-pitched echo and look up to see Eeek charging in our direction.

Everyone stood back, like the parting of the waves. It was clear Eeek was heading straight for Cameron Hicks. You should have seen the look of terror in Hicksy's eyes! Eeek's mad grin can't have helped.

'Here comes my second cousin,' I faltered.
Eeek pounced on Cameron, wrapped his green arms around him and began smothering him in kisses!

'Hey, hold back, Myles!' I cried, pulling at Eeek's arm. 'Sorry, Hicksy, cousin Myles gets carried away sometimes. You know, acting type.' Cameron, gasping for breath, had by now collapsed on the ground where Eeek proceeded to dive on top of him, blue smoke billowing from his ears.

'Check out those special effects!' someone said.

'He'll have Hicksy for lunch!' said another.

Finally I managed to disentangle Eeek from Cameron Hicks who looked so pale when he stood up he resembled an alien himself.

I pulled Eeek to one side and muttered angrily to him about getting us all into trouble. He seemed to understand and quickly retired in disgrace to the sideline while I made excuses to the referee. Cameron was a changed person after that. He kept staring over his shoulder at Eeek with a bizarre look in his eyes. Who could blame him?

Jake's dad had, surprise surprise, missed the whole episode. But then again, if you'd asked him what colours the two teams had been wearing that morning he wouldn't have been able to answer you.

The car ride home was quiet. Eeek had disappeared into the trees. We would have to have a serious talk when I got home.

Seven

Perhaps not so surprisingly, Eeek *wasn't* in my room when I returned.

'He's sulking,' I said to Jake. I pretended I didn't care.

That afternoon I went off to the park with Dad, Rory and Jake to play cricket. (Well, you know, Rory ran around getting in our way, hi-jacking the ball and generally causing trouble while we tried to play cricket.)

When I got home Eeek still wasn't there.

Then Mum asked me where my school tracksuit bottoms were. See what I mean about her sixth sense? Why, this week of all weeks, does she decide we should pack my sports things for Monday on *Sunday afternoon?* Normally we're both racing around at two minutes to eight on a Monday morning trying to get everything together.

'No idea where they are,' I said ultra vaguely. 'I'll look properly later.'

That seemed to do the trick and she didn't ask again.

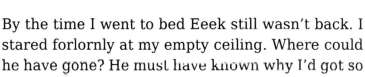

By the time I went to bed Eeek still wasn't back. I stared forlornly at my empty ceiling. Where could he have gone? He must have known why I'd got so angry with him. Had he gone home? To visit another Earth child? Maybe he was watching me on his little TV screen? *His TV screen!*

I scrambled from my bed and switched on the light. It was two o'clock in the morning and I hadn't slept. I turned my room upside down but, to my horror, the suitcase was gone. So were all of Eeek's belongings. I went back to bed, my cheeks burning. *How could he have done it?* Disappeared without even saying goodbye! I switched off the light as the tears welled up in my eyes. Then as my head hit the pillow I heard a gentle 'rat tat tat' on my windowpane.

A full moon lit up the sky. I hadn't bothered to close my curtains. There, pressed up against the glass, was a grinning green face.

'Where have you been?' I whispered in a high pitch as I opened the window.

With his little suitcase in hand and still wearing my tracksuit bottoms, trainers and Northbridge United scarf, Eeek climbed in off the window ledge.

He stood face to face with me and gave a funny look that was half sad and half happy then started to blink very slowly. 'You look tired!' I said. Eeek tossed a glance to his sleeping place on the ceiling and let out a massive yawn. There was no point trying to talk to him now. He was ready for bed.

It was hard for me to get to sleep after that, even though I was exhausted. I kept squinting up through the darkness to check for Eeek's silhouette above.

But soon he began to snore. That helped I think, because the next thing I knew Mum was calling that it was time to get up.

As I sat up in bed I was astonished to find that Eeek had tidied my whole room again. I was grateful for this as I'd left it in a real mess after my hunt for his case. Still, I thought, it probably only took him a couple of seconds!

'Morning!' I said brightly, pulling my clothes on. Eeek was sitting at my desk studying something on his TV screen. He turned and grinned widely, as if to say, 'I'm glad you've forgiven me.'

'Come on, Charlie!' shouted Mum.

'Eeek, I have to go to school,' I said. 'Will you be here when I get back?' Eeek nodded and I believed him. I picked up my tracksuit bottoms, which Eeek had left folded on the end of my bed, and hurtled downstairs.

Eight

The behaviour of my 'second cousin' Myles was the talk of our class that day. 'Fancy spending your weekend dressed up as an alien!' said Fred Posslethwaite.

'My dad said there's a name for people like him!' said Arthur Chatty, sniggering.

Then the questions started. What was this science fiction children's programme? How did he do the blue smoke thing? Which acting school did Myles go to? And so on. Most worrying, Sid Spiker, my creepy neighbour from out the back, who happens to be a real sci-fi fanatic, wanted to know every last detail about my 'alleged cousin'.

What was his outfit made of? Who was his agent? Did he have to carry a fire certificate? Could he come and interview him for 'Sci-Fi Weekly'?

The news also spread to the girls, who gathered in small groups and began whispering and pointing at me. This made an interesting change. It was normally Cameron Hicks 'the soccer hero' they all giggled over.

Sophie Marr, the poshest girl in our class, had declared her undying love for Cameron in three love letters. We all teased him something rotten about it. I suppose we were a bit jealous. Not because we liked girls of course, just 'cause none of them fancied us.

Out of everyone, Cameron stayed surprisingly quiet that morning. In fact, he still had a pasty alien look about his face. Had Eeek cast an alien spell on him, I wondered? I was worried.

Nine

My fears about Sid Spiker were confirmed when he started sending me texts after school saying he 'knew' about the alien. Of course I didn't reply – and I let my mobile phone go to voicemail when he tried calling.

But then , after supper, he telephoned our house out of the blue. Just my luck to pick up.

'I know about the alien,' he murmured darkly.

'What are you talking about?' I said quickly, darting a glance down the hallway to check for Mum.

'Don't waste my time, Charlie Spruit. I've seen him! On your window ledge last night. All green and glowing like a stick insect!'

I swear my heart skipped about 50 beats. True, Sid's garden does back onto the end of ours, but how could he have seen that far? It's at least 100 metres from his bedroom window to mine – and there's a tree in between! Anyway, why would he

44

be looking out *at two o'clock in the morning* on a Sunday night?

Sid breathed menacingly down the phone, waiting for my reply.

'Don't talk rubbish,' I snorted weakly. Just then I remembered his telescope.

'Saw him through me telescope!' he rasped. 'Full moon last night, weren't it? Got way more than I bargained for when I got up to check it though, didn't I, eh?' He sniggered smugly.

I tried to force a reply but my mind went blank.

'Here's the deal,' he sniffed. '24 hours with your slimy friend and I keep my mouth shut. *Otherwise* I tell the newspapers.'

'No way, Spiker!' I blurted out. 'And, for your information, he's *no way slimy!*'

I pressed the disconnect button so hard it nearly disappeared inside the phone.

'Are you all right, dear?'

Mum had appeared behind me, her timing, as usual, spot on. I smiled sweetly then dashed up the stairs.

'Sid Spiker's onto you,' I said as I slammed my bedroom door behind me.

Eeek looked up from reading 'England Football: A Complete History' and gave a puzzled frown.

Then I nearly jumped out of my skin as the house phone, which was still in my sweaty hand, rang again.

'You're playing dangerous games,' Sid croaked.

'Get lost, Spiker!' I shouted down the receiver. 'On *Mars* preferably!'

'You'll live to regret this,' he whispered, just before I cut him off again. Perhaps I should have listened.

On Wednesday Sid Spiker started giving me funny looks across the classroom and winking at me whenever he passed. This was a mean form of torment.

I warned Eeek to keep away from the window and banned any future outings. Spiker's a serious sci-fi weirdo. He'd do anything to get himself on the front page of 'Sci-Fi Weekly'. I wouldn't put kidnapping past Sid Spiker - nor, come to think of it, murder. His whole family's pretty weird. Everyone says his big brother Norman surfs the Internet talking to serial killers.

Eeek was luckily quite happy to stay 'home alone' that week while I was at school. He spent his time watching the build-up to Friday night's England-Brazil match on his little TV screen. Jake and I had told him we'd watch it with him in my room and he was obviously looking forward to being with proper (AKA human!) England fans for once!

Whenever anyone entered the room Eeek miraculously disappeared - except, of course, if it was Jake. Rory, who was convinced I was harbouring an alien, randomly dived through my door without warning. But Eeek always managed to outsmart him, and between us we all rather enjoyed this game of 'alien' cat and mouse.

Eeek never got hungry or thirsty. Nor did he seem to need the loo! It was a pretty cool partnership all in all - especially since he kept tidying my room!

Ten

Friday was the day of the big match, but when I got back from school I was alarmed to find my alien friend had disappeared again.

By seven o'clock Eeek still hadn't reappeared and by the time Jake arrived fifteen minutes before kick-off I was seriously worried.

'Where is he? He's going to miss the match!' I muttered, pacing up and down like a worried father.

'Cool it, Charlie,' said Jake, laughing. 'He's probably gone to the match!'

The blood drained from my cheeks.

With butterflies in my tummy and my throat already tightening I dashed to Eeek's little case, which was still sitting on my desk. As I flung open the lid my fears were confirmed. The airline ticket and the England Supporters' Club membership card were missing!

'He *has* gone to the match!' I shouted. 'I don't

believe it!'

By now it was five to eight. We thundered down the stairs to catch the kick-off with Dad and Rory.

Waves of anger and fear swept over me in turns as we sat down. On the one hand I was hurt and very cross at my friend for going off like that without telling me, especially as we'd planned to watch the match together. On the other, I felt really protective towards him. Eeek was putting himself in danger and I knew if anything happened to him I'd never forgive myself for not stopping him. But there was nothing I could do - except wait and hope.

The first half got off to such a bizarre start I was convinced it was all Eeek's doing. Two penalties in ten minutes! The first against England for a *goalkeeper foul?!* (I think not!) The second against Brazil for a filthy tackle on Carraber inside the penalty box.

Steve Mitchell strutted his stuff, of course, and with the score at 1-1 we'd each nearly had two heart attacks inside ten minutes.

As the match settled down, Jake and I sat on the carpet in a sort of trance, lurching forward trying to spot Eeek each time the camera panned across the crowds.

'What *are* you two doing?' said Dad finally.

'They're looking for that alien who lives in Charlie's room!' shouted Rory, bouncing up and down on the sofa. 'He's gone to the match! I saw him!'

I swivelled round and stared at Rory, my face a dark shade of beetroot. Jake was suddenly joking on his peanut beside me. Had Rory seen Eeek go out?

'You're a laugh a minute, Rory!' said Dad, with one of his annoying chuckles.

Jake and I swapped sideways glances then carried on watching the match.

As the minutes ticked by England put on a superb performance, bolstered by supreme defending from Peter Hinx and Damien Cole and a run of awesome crosses from Joe Carraber and Tom Hale.

Then, just before half time, star striker Steve Mitchell flicked the ball from under the heels of the Brazilian defender, ran a third of the way down the pitch and scored a beauty top left into the net from 50 yards. *2-1!*

The England fans went crazy. Rory, Jake and Dad screamed so loud I thought my eardrums would burst. It was then that I spotted familiar blue smoke rising from the grandstand off to the left.

As my eyes froze in their sockets I slowly began to hyperventilate.

Seconds after Steve Mitchell's goal hit the back of the net the term 'pitch invasion' took on a new meaning. A camera immediately picked up Eeek who was already charging down the grandstand towards the pitch.

'Oh, I say, and it looks like we have a streaker coming our way!' shouted the commentator. 'And an *alien* streaker at that!'

The England fans let out a roar as Eeek streaked onto the pitch with wafts of blue smoke trailing in his wake.

'There he is! There he is!' screeched Rory, his cheeks as red as a tomato.

The stewards, who obviously knew trouble when they saw it, came racing out from all directions to try and block Eeek's path to Steve Mitchell.

With his back to Eeek, Mitchell was at least spared the ordeal of knowing what was about to happen. Eeek easily out-dodged the stewards and within a couple of seconds had jumped on Steve Mitchell's back and started smothering his neck with kisses.

'Well, this really is silly season stuff!' muttered the reporter.

'I'll say, Brian!' chuckled his colleague. They were obviously both in need of a pair of glasses.

Rory was now bouncing up and down so hard on the sofa I was sure his head would go crashing through the ceiling. Dad's smile, meanwhile, slowly turned to a frown. As for Jake and me, well we bit our lips hard and kept our heads low.

When finally Steve Mitchell emerged from the throng of stewards his face was a strange green colour. In fact, not unlike Cameron's the week before at football practice. The last we saw of Eeek was his wafts of blue smoke rising high above the heads of two policemen who had appeared to help escort him off the pitch.

After the match, Eeek made it onto the ten o'clock news – the bit at the end where they do the funny stories.

'There he is!' screeched Rory, by now delirious with fatigue. (It was three hours past his usual bedtime.) As Eeek once again raced out from the crowds, the newsreader described him as a 'rogue alien streaker' who had managed to 'slip the net' of the police (AKA escape!) shortly after being escorted off the pitch.

Suggestions that it had been a 'real live alien' were put down to 'crowd hysteria' on the one hand and 'excuses for poor policing' on the other. The news channel, meanwhile, had been flooded with calls from across the country about alien sightings, UFOs and green shooting stars, all somehow connected with England striker Steve Mitchell.

I felt a mixture of relief, worry and anger as I went to bed that night. At least Eeek had managed to get away from the police. But where had he gone to now?

Eleven

By Saturday morning I was like a walking zombie. I'd spent most of the night peering at my window, listening in vain for Eeek's 'rat tat tat'. I'm not sure what time I finally dozed off but I was later woken, by the sound of Dad's raised voice, from a bizarre dream in which I was *dancing* with my alien friend. I forced myself up, grabbed my dressing gown and went downstairs.

As I came into the kitchen Dad sat sternly on the far side of the breakfast table, his eyebrows like crossed samurai swords.

'What's up, Dad?' I said in a high voice. I had no

idea what was wrong, but for some reason couldn't help feeling guilty. Maybe he'd found out about that £5 I 'borrowed' from the hall table the other week and forgot to mention to anyone. Great - that was all I needed right now! I really had meant to pay it back.

Dad leaned forward and pushed a piece of paper in front of me that looked like a bank statement.

I glanced at the boring list of entries. 'What's this?' I asked, my voice still guiltily high. I was trying to see if anything on the statement said £5, but wasn't having any luck. (Mind you, why the money I had borrowed from the hall table would have been on Dad's bank statement I have no idea – I was obviously panicking.)

'There, son!' said Dad between clenched teeth. He jabbed a finger about half way down the page. 'Someone used my credit card to buy a ticket to last night's match! Cheek of it!'

And now, as I focused my weary eyes, I read the following entry:

'World Cup Wicked Tickets'
England/Brazil 1 x ticket @ £400'

Just at that moment Rory swaggers in. 'Why was Daddy shouting at Charlie?' he asked with a smug grin.

'He wasn't,' said Mum, putting a boiled egg on the table in front of me. Rory looked disappointed.

'Someone's been very bad and used Daddy's credit card to buy a World Cup ticket,' Mum went on.

Rory's eyes immediately lit up. 'I know who it was!' he shrieked. 'It was that alien from Charlie's room! I saw him with the ticket the other morning when everyone was asleep!'

We all stared at Rory in silence.

'And look!' he said with a wide grin. 'He gave me a miniature Red Arrows plane!'

Mum chuckled at Rory then pinched his cheeks as I almost inhaled my egg.

As I sat there my anger started to well. So *that* was the purpose of Eeek's visit! He had used my dad's credit card number to get hold of a ticket to the World Cup! My so-called 'friend' had used me to further his own interest in football! This was utterly and totally unforgivable. With my eyes smarting I stomped up the stairs to my room. I felt tired and upset - not to mention extremely angry. You can therefore imagine my annoyed surprise when I lay back down on my bed to find Eeek grinning down at me from the ceiling - just as if he'd never left.

Twelve

'I can't believe you!' I cried angrily, as he walked coolly across the ceiling, down my wall and stepped onto the carpet. 'Do you have any idea what you've done? You've stolen from my parents and you've used me! *And* you've made a complete idiot of yourself in front of 150 million people! Do you realise you could have been taken away by the government laboratory? What would I have told your parents then?' (Talking of parents, I was beginning to sound like one.)

Eeek studied the floor and blinked slowly.

'And what about poor Steve Mitchell?' I went on. 'You might have given him a heart attack!'

Things were starting to get out of hand and I was cross. 'I'm sorry, Eeek, but I think you'd better go back home before I get into trouble and you get caught and locked away.'

Tears were now welling in Eeek's eyes and he was shaking his head vigorously.

'Telephone, Charlie!' Mum was calling up the stairs.

'*Don't* go away!' I said, glaring, and dashed out.

'Why's your mobile's switched off? Any news?' It was Jake.

'He's back,' I whispered.

'Great! I'll come round!'

When I got back to my room Eeek was sitting on my bed crying again! The cheek of it! How dare he?! I took a deep breath trying to think of what to say next, when in storms Jake waving a thin piece of card in the air.

'Post for you, Eeek!' he cries, gleefully, then barges right past me and thrusts the card into Eeek's slender luminous fingers.

Sophie Marr requests the pleasure of your company
at her 12th Birthday Party
on
Saturday 19 July 7-10pm
St Michael's Hall
Disco. Fancy Dress. Entertainment
Be There
or
Be Square

'What's this?' I muttered angrily.

As Eeek's glistening eyes moved slowly down the

card his mouth widened into a grin.

'We've all got one!' Jake said, pulling two more cards from his pocket and tossing one in my direction. As I read the words on the invitation I did so with mixed emotions.

'"*Requests the pleasure of your company,*"!' I sneered. 'Who does she think she is, The Queen?

'What's more,' I said with a scowl, 'that's tonight. How come we've been invited last minute?'

'Cousin "Myles", of course,' chuckled Jake. 'Sophie's desperate to meet him. Especially after last night's football. Aliens are all the rage now. Looks like Cameron Hicks is right off her hit list!'

Immediately Eeek's pale pink eyes lit up.

I raised my eyes to the ceiling. 'Sophie Marr is a girl you know, Eeek!'

Eeek smiled and widened his eyes further, which made me rather worried.

'Anyway, he can't go!' I said, remembering myself.

'Why not?' said Jake.

'Because he's stolen from my parents!' I said firmly. 'Eeek's going home this morning, aren't you, Eeek?'

At this Eeek burst into tears again making me look the real ogre. Don't ask me why, but I sort of felt sorry for him.

After much discussion, a lot of alien sobbing, and quite a bit of arguing between me and Jake, it was finally agreed that Eeek could stay and come to the party if he promised that:

1) He would stick by me at all times.
2) He would head home to his family straight afterwards.

Thirteen

Saturday evening. 6.30pm. Jake and I had squeezed into our lime green all-in-one lycra ski thermals, borrowed from Lucinda Hextall-Smythe's twin girls earlier that day. (Lucinda's my mum's poshest friend at the health club.) Mum had plastered us with white facemask cream, blue lipstick and red and green hairspray. In case you hadn't guessed, we were going as aliens.

I had had several pep talks with Eeek who promised not to try anything silly.

At seven o'clock Eeek left by my window and Jake and I set off. Eeek seemed to know where he needed to go and we trusted him.

As we reached St Michael's Hall Eeek appeared from around a corner looking more alien-like than ever. He seemed to have turned up his voltage or scrubbed his skin or something. Whatever it was, he suddenly looked a whole lot more luminous than when we left him.

'Cool alien, mate!' cried a passing hunchback. A Dracula, a gladiator and a pirate all gasped at the haze of green light emanating from Eeek's silhouette.

'Turn it down!' I muttered walking in. 'And remember to watch out for Sid Spiker!' I didn't think for a minute Sophie would have invited Sid but was feeling kind of paranoid.

You should have seen the look on Sophie Marr's face when we sauntered into the hall. '*You* must be the famous Myles!' she cooed as we handed over birthday gifts like the three wise men.

Eeek nodded and smiled in silence while Sophie flashed her big brown eyes at him. I have to admit she did look pretty dazzling in her black Catgirl outfit. That is, the outfit looked pretty dazzling I mean.

Sophie was clearly waiting for an answer from Eeek. 'He's still in role play,' I faltered, trying not to stare. 'Been filming all day. Doesn't talk.' Sophie blushed after us in admiration as we were swept into the hall with the other guests.

Immediately I felt edgy about Sid Spiker and darted my eyes through the crowds, trying to see if he was there in disguise. Eeek, meanwhile, began craning his neck across the heads then, quite suddenly, started grinning and puffing blue smoke.

I followed his gaze into the corner where I was alarmed to see Cameron Hicks staring back at him. Even more disturbing was that Hicksy was dressed as Eeek's all-time favourite - England Striker *Steve Mitchell!* Name, number 9 shirt and all!

I was just starting to panic and look around for Jake, who had disappeared, when the crowd broke into spontaneous applause and surged towards the stage. Eeek switched his gaze to the front.

Sophie Marr's family never does anything by halves and this was no exception. Sophie's mum had apparently hired the most expensive entertainer in London and the most famous DJ in southeast England. I wouldn't be surprised if she'd also hired the Queen's caterers.

After leading a chorus of 'Happy Birthday', 'Tricky Dicky' opened with a five-pin juggling routine that left us all gasping for breath. Even Eeek couldn't take his eyes off the slender white skittles as they flew one after the other up into the rafters only to be deftly caught on the way down, then hurled right back up again.

After the routine ended, Tricky Dicky bowed and we all clapped. He then went on to spin plates, juggle eggs and eat fire - while I kept half an eye on my alien friend, just in case he had any 'bright' ideas.

As Tricky Dicky took his last sweeping bow, I breathed a sigh of relief. At least Eeek hadn't tried anything on. But then, just as the audience began to applaud - and worries of Sid Spiker came creeping back into my mind - the roll of drums echoed around the hall.

'And for my *final* act,' said the magician grinning widely, obviously pleased to have caught us all out, 'I need an *extra special* volunteer!'

A flash of white light streaked across the stage, momentarily blinding us all. Seconds later the crowds started cheering, as, to my horror, a familiar lime green silhouette emerged through the clouds of blue smoke now billowing up in front of us. Extra special. Extraterrestrial. Looking back, I suppose they do sort of sound the same.

Fourteen

Tricky Dicky tried hard not to look surprised at Eeek's translucent green body and grinning moon-shaped face. 'My, oh, my!' he chortled uneasily. 'Certainly never made outfits like that in my day!' Eeek smiled confidently and bowed to the audience who all cheered heartily. I suppose they thought he was part of the act.

'*What the heck's he up to?*' Jake was suddenly at my ear.

'Don't ask me,' I grumbled. 'Where have you been anyway?'

Jake was about to reply when the magician started up again.

'*So* we have an alien with us!' Tricky Dicky laughed uneasily again. 'Welcome to our planet Earth, Mr Alien! **C-a-n y-o-u t-e-l-l u-s y-o-u-r n-a-m-e?**'

Jake and I groaned and covered our faces.

'*Eeek!*' screeched Eeek at the top of his voice.

Tricky Dicky clapped his hands to his ears as the audience cheered some more.

Eeek, meanwhile, began blinking enthusiastically in the direction of the front row of the audience, and as I peered through the onlookers' heads I quickly spotted Sophie Marr at the edge of the stage with Cameron Hicks in his Steve Mitchell football strip nudging up next to her.

Hicksy was either genuinely in love or had been dared to try and put his arm around Sophie. Bad news for him, though, because she instantly pushed him away. Sophie only had eyes for Eeek now and, by the looks of things, Eeek only had eyes for her too.

'Now, girls and boys,' said Tricky Dicky when the crowds had finally calmed, 'how would you like to see an alien *sawn in half*?'

This sent the audience back into a frenzy, all clapping and stamping their feet. As the commotion resonated around the hall droplets of sweat began surfacing through my face cream making my brow feel like diluted toothpaste. Eeek, meanwhile, continued grinning in Sophie Marr's direction, which I found more than a little irritating.

Tricky Dicky disappeared briefly into the wings and reappeared wheeling a long low table on which a coffin-shaped box sat with its lid open. He gave Eeek a stiff grin.

'Now, my friend, perhaps you would like to step

inside my box?'

Eeek bowed proudly to the audience, then strolled over and climbed inside, all the time straining his neck round in Sophie Marr's direction.

The magician slowly lowered the lid and draped a black velvet cover over the top. Eeek's moon-shaped face now grinned out of one end, while his translucent spindly feet wriggled out of the other.

'Drums please!' shouted Tricky Dicky. Someone in the wings flicked a switch and as the drums began to roll the crowd fell eerily silent. Then, from inside his cloak, Tricky Dicky whisked out a stainless-steel saw with shark-like teeth that glinted in the spotlights.

Horrified, I pushed forward through the crowds, tears of white sweat now trickling down my cheeks. Sophie Marr clapped her hand to her mouth while Cameron Hicks, beside her, craned forward, trying to get a better look. Eeek, meanwhile, carried on puffing out blue smoke and smiling like a lovesick parrot.

As the saw cut into the wood I held my breath and splayed my sticky fingers across my eyes. Surely Eeek would try something now? But, no, as the saw appeared to cut right through the box his grin remained unchanged.

With his task complete Tricky Dicky threw down his saw, pulled off the velvet cloth, and turned to the audience in triumph.

The sound system crackled out a trumpet fanfare and the first ripples of applause broke out. It was then that somebody noticed.

'Hey, how d'ya do that then?'

The magician's smarmy grin dissolved as he shot a puzzled glance out into the audience.

'Those toes are still moving, look!'

Tricky Dicky swivelled his head to look behind him as a wave of inward gasps echoed right around the hall.

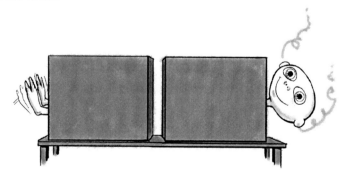

The voice that had noticed was right.

You see, the box containing Eeek had divided in the centre and now had a clear gap separating each half.

More worrying than this, though, was that Eeek's wriggling green feet remained in the left-hand section, while his lovesick face still grinned out at Sophie Marr from the right.

At that moment the hall plunged into darkness. A few people started to clap. Others, less certain, started whispering.

'What's going on!' screamed Sophie Marr.

'Get the lights!' screamed someone else.

After a brief commotion the lights flashed back on. The magician stood in a daze. Then, with his face a sickly white colour, he began bowing out hastily, only to trip backwards over one half of the black box which now lay empty on the stage floor. The audience shrieked with laughter as his fall delivered him into a crumpled heap beneath his cloak. I, meanwhile, flashed my eyes around in a panic. Not only had Eeek disappeared, but so had *Cameron Hicks!*

'Eeek's kidnapped Hicksy!' I shrieked at Jake. 'He probably thinks he's really Steve Mitchell!'

'What *are* you ranting on about?' said Jake, as if I'd just gone loony. 'Hicksy's still over there!' He grabbed me by the shoulders and turned me to face the corner where Eeek had spotted Cameron when we first arrived.

And now, as my eyes fell on Cameron Hicks still larking about with his friends dressed as Steve Mitchell, a ghastly feeling crept over me.

'So who the *heck* was the Steve Mitchell who was with Sophie—?' I gasped.

'Where's that creep gone?' Sophie was suddenly upon me, flashing her great eyelashes and twirling her black cat's tail menacingly.

'What creep?' I spluttered, going red. The DJ put on the first record.

'Sid Spiker, of course!' she bellowed. 'First he gatecrashes my party disguised as Steve Mitchell, then he tries to flirt with me - next thing he goes off with your cousin!'

In panic I clutched Jake's arm. But Jake had collapsed into laughter.

'Sid Spiker dressed as *Steve Mitchell!?*' he shrieked. 'Now *that's* what I call funny! Spiker wouldn't know a football if it hit him on the nose!'

Jake, as you've probably just worked out, wouldn't spot a crisis inside an erupting volcano.

'Shut up, Jake!' shouted Sophie above the music. 'This is *my* birthday party and *you* were meant to introduce me to Myles. *Where's* Sid Spiker taken him?'

'The newspapers!' I screeched in horror. I grasped Jake's arm and started dragging him towards the door.

Sophie Marr, who had a look of desperation about her, was quickly surrounded by a group of friends who tried to calm her down. Jake and I bolted out into the night as the disco music was turned up a level.

Fifteen

When we got to Sid's house the lights were all on. Jake reached up and pressed the doorbell while I furiously rubbed the side of my itching nose. My face cream was dissolving and I was sweating all over. Meanwhile, Lucinda Hextall-Smythe's now green-and-white-streaked thermals seemed to have fused to my body.

Norman Spiker answered the door clutching a half-eaten hot dog. Norman is Sid's slimy big brother. He's got zits the size of Smarties and only washes his hair once a year.

'So, who have we here?' he cackled, running his chubby fingers through his greasy locks. 'A couple of melting aliens, eh?' He raised his eyebrows and grinned, exposing yellow teeth with pieces of onion lodged in between.

'Hey, Sidney!' he bellowed, breathing frankfurter all over me. 'More aliens at the door! Doing group interviews tonight are we?'

Sid Spiker, still in his Steve Mitchell strip, emerged at the top of the stairs.

'What d'ya want, Spruit?' he said sharply. He clearly had no intention of coming down.

'I've come for my - *friend*,' I stammered.

Norman burped into the air then winked at me.

'Dunno *what* you're talking about!' replied Sid. He folded his arms and smirked triumphantly down at us. 'Now, if you don't mind, I'm busy.'

I forced my words out, glancing at Jake for support. 'Now look here, Spiker, don't play games with me! He's got special powers you know. If you upset him you never know—'

'Give it a rest, kid!' Norman pierced me with a dark stare as he chased a piece of food round his mouth with his tongue. 'If Sid says your friend's not here, that means he's *not here*. Geddit?' He tore off a bite of his hot dog and began chewing menacingly, then gave me another wink as Sid turned and disappeared out of sight.

'Let me speak to your mum!' I challenged.

'She's out! Now you two just scarper, hear me?' Norman's evil eyes suddenly widened. '*Otherwise I'll let Nipper out!*'

I went to open my mouth but Norman slammed the door in my face.

Jake was already halfway down the garden path. As I followed him towards the gate a lump began travelling up my throat. Sid was sure to hand Eeek over to the newspapers. After that he wouldn't stand a chance, and I'd probably never see him again!

Jake grabbed me by the arm and started running. 'Come on, Charlie, let's get out of here. Eeek'll find his own way out.'

In case you're wondering, Nipper's the Spiker family's bull terrier. Sid calls him Fang for short. Oh, yes, and in case you hadn't guessed, Jake's petrified of dogs.

Sixteen

Jake was staying at my house that night. Armed with my binoculars and telescope, we quickly set up stall by my bedroom window, which looks down the garden to the back of Sid's house.

At half past eleven Mum and Dad went to bed. Ten minutes later Norman appeared at the Spikers' back door to let out the dog. Nipper's a mean-looking beast. Not the sort you want to come across on a lonely afternoon stroll. His muzzle only comes off at night when he sleeps in his kennel in the back garden. As you might imagine, Jake and I had no immediate plans to scale the fence.

Just before midnight the lights at the Spiker house finally started switching off. Soon the whole house was in darkness - except, that is, for Sid's window where an ominous green glow filtered through the curtains.

'What's that creep up to?' I whispered in panic.

Shadows scuttled back and forth behind the curtains; lights occasionally flashed. Of course! Sid was taking photographs to try to sell to the newspapers! As I stared through my telescope, my hands sticky with face cream, I was sickened to think of Spiker using Eeek to get his name into Sci-Fi Weekly. He'd probably sell his story to the national newspapers too. Spiker would stoop to anything to get famous. That's the sad kind of person he is.

Jake stood yawning beside me, all green and white streaked, like my twin. 'It'll be fine!' he sighed, lowering the binoculars, then went and lay down on my bed.

'Not there! You're sleeping on the Z-bed!' I remonstrated. 'Anyway, you can't go to sleep now!'

But Jake was already dozing off.

For the next five minutes I stayed glued (almost literally) to the window - even though I couldn't see anything. Then, just when I thought he was asleep, Jake suddenly yells out 'Hey!' almost giving me a heart attack.

I swung round in alarm. Before I could shout 'watch that shelf' my best friend sat up and cracked his head - WHACK! - right on the corner.

'The little TV screen!' he gasped with a drunken grin, then slumped back down on his back. This was one of Jake's rare moments of vision. Unfortunately he wasn't conscious to share it.

Luckily Jake came round within a few seconds and as he now lay groaning and rubbing his head I rifled under my bed for Eeek's case. Moments later we were sitting on the carpet staring into Eeek's little TV screen which had already started to illuminate.

Despite the bump on his head Jake deciphered the emerging image much faster than I did.

'It's the alien parents from Eeek's photo!' he screeched in delight. He was right. The picture that slowly came into focus showed two adult aliens staring straight out at us. In fact it looked very much as if they'd been *waiting* for us.

My heart immediately began to race. 'D'you think they can they see us?' I said, my voice quivering.

'*I* dunno. Let's say something.'

But then, unable to stop myself, I lunged forward and twirled the dials.

'What are you *doing*?' said Jake in a fury. The aliens disappeared from the screen.

'We've *got* to rescue Eeek first!' I heard myself cry. 'I can't tell them he's been *kidnapped* by a sci-fi fanatic! They'll probably *zap* me!' To my surprise, I was trembling all over.

Jake sat smarting as I proceeded to flick like a madman through a host of terrestrial TV channels; American, Spanish, Russian, Australian, Japanese - before finally reaching a band of darkness.

'This could be it!' I whispered in hope. I was somehow sure we would be able to tune into Eeek. But then, as I continued turning the dials, only silent blackness confronted us, and after five minutes I knew we had more chance of spotting a fly in the dark than of finding an alien lost on a wavelength. Until, that is, Jake spotted it.

'How about this!' he said with a grin, as he deftly pulled up an aerial from the top right-hand corner of the screen. This was another of Jake's 'moments', and one for which I will be forever grateful. Immediately we began to get a signal. Seconds later we got sound.

'Get on with it!' we heard an angry voice yell.

'It's Spiker!' whispered Jake in a frenzy. A fuzzy picture began to take shape, like two frogmen in an underwater snowstorm. I glanced across to Sid's window. The glow was a flickering green.

'*E-e-e-k!*' we heard Eeek screech in terror.

'He's torturing him!' I yelled in panic. Furiously I tried to focus the picture, spinning the dials left then right and back again. Then suddenly, 'Eureka!' we had them - clear as crystal in front of us.

Seventeen

Unbelievably, Sid Spiker and Eeek were sitting with their backs against a bed surrounded by *empty Red Bull cans!* Spiker was just downing the last drops from one, while Eeek was opening another. Both of them seemed to be looking at a bank of flashing lights somewhere just out of view.

'They're getting *hyper* on Red Bull!' I gasped in horror. 'I know all about that stuff. Will Austin's teenage brother drinks it when he's late with his homework – says the caffeine in it keeps you awake for days!'

'What's all that flashing?' said Jake with a frown.

As if someone had heard us, the screen instantly switched to point in the direction of the flashes.

'It's a telly!' said Jake, jumping up. 'They're watching telly!'

I pressed the zoom button and narrowed my eyes to focus. I could barely believe it: England v Germany 1966 World Cup Final. A classic! I zoomed in some more. A pile of DVDs marked 'Match of the Day' sat at the base of the television. I panned back. Now looking all around I could see England flags and posters covering Sid Spiker's bedroom walls.

'That sneaky creep!' I breathed. 'Spiker's pretending he's a football fan! He *hates* sport!'
See what I mean? Spiker would stoop to anything for his moment of fame.

'What's that?' said Jake, suddenly pointing. A fainter white light was flickering off in one corner. Instantly the little TV screen image switched - once again as if someone had heard us.

'It's another telly!' said Jake.

But already I could see he was wrong.

'No it's not!' I said. 'It's a laptop!'

At that moment I had a strange thought – almost like someone was controlling my mind. I lunged at the zoom button to take a closer look at the laptop screen.

There staring out at us was the World Cup logo.

Underneath, in bright red letters, a flashing sign read as follows:

World Cup Wicked Tickets
Get Yours Here! £400 Free Local Delivery!
Managing Director: Norman G. Spiker

'Norman Spiker!' I gasped. 'Sid's brother, the Internet hacker!'

Slowly I sat back in shock – not to mention guilt. Because at that moment I realised that it wasn't Eeek who had used my dad's credit card details to get his match ticket! It must have been Sid's creepy big brother, Norman. He must have hacked into Dad's account to buy the ticket and then sold it to Eeek somehow!

'Right, that's it!' I screeched, jumping up.

'You can't go over!' said Jake, his voice shaking. 'What about Nipper?' I know it sounds impossible, but Jake's white-streaked face was turning visibly whiter with each word.

'I'm not *that* stupid!' I said, rolling my eyes. (Jake really should know me better.) I triumphantly held up my phone. 'Two can play at texting, don't you know!'

Within 15 seconds I had composed my message:

'Hey creep! I know ur brother hacked in2 my dad's bank account! U let Eeek go quietly NOW or I call the cops!'

I beamed as I studied my work of genius. But my smile quickly turned to a frown. I'd typed **'caps'** not **'cops'**! Darn!

Sid was quick to reply:

'Forget it! I ain't thaat stooopid! U call the CAPS (ha! ha!) and your alien friend ends up at the government lab.'

Of course I had no intention of calling the police - I knew better than to risk getting Eeek caught, but it seemed to worry Sid because moments later he opened the back door and stuck his head out, as if listening for sirens. He then smirked in the direction of my bedroom window, waved triumphantly and shut the door.

Seeing his smarmy face through my telescope filled me with fury. 'On second thoughts, I *am* going over!' I said angrily. I grabbed my cricket bat for defence against Nipper and opened the door. Jake, to my surprise, followed me as I tiptoed down the stairs. He obviously had great faith in my dog-batting skills, despite the fact I only ever bat last man!

As it turned out, we needn't have worried about Nipper because once we got over the fence into the garden he didn't, as we expected, rouse from his kennel to attack us. In fact he was snoring so loudly I thought he might wake the neighbours!

We sidled around the edge of the garden to the back door and tried the handle. Genius! Sid had forgotten to lock it! In we snuck and crept up the stairs through the dark to Sid's room. As I pressed my ear against the door, muffled gasps, laughs and the sound of football commentary filtered through.

My heart was racing. 'I'm going in!' I whispered. I raised my cricket bat in the air with one hand, and flung open the door with the other.

You should have seen the look on Sid's and Eeek's faces seeing us standing there. Sid's dark-eyed scowl would make a psychopathic murderer look like your best friend. In contrast, Eeek's expression of startled delight, topped off with a mouth-to-ear grin and jets of blue ear-smoke seemed to say 'Hi, guys! Come and join the fun!'

I was just trying to work out my next move (I've never been that good at planning...) when the stench of cooked onion floated over my left shoulder.

'*Oi*! What are you two doing here?'

Jake and I swivelled round just in time to glimpse Norman Spiker's menacing stare - before a blinding white flash filled the air.

Eighteen

When the light faded, I found myself blinking wide-eyed in Sid's doorway still standing next to Jake. There was no sign of Norman and Sid was now sitting alone staring in an open-mouthed trance in the direction of his telly. At first I couldn't see Eeek, but then spotted a green glow coming from under Sid's bed.

'What's going on—' I started crossly, as we entered Sid's bedroom.

'Where's Eeek?' cut in Jake glancing all around and up at the ceiling. Jake's never been very observant. That's why he's never beaten me at chess.

'Check this out!' Sid whispered, in a kind of panicked awe.

Jake and I swiveled round to see a dark-haired woman and a blonde-haired man dressed in silver spacesuits - like from Star Trek or Star Wars or something - smiling out at us from Sid's telly. The telly itself was giving off a fluorescent glow, as if it had been taken over.

'What the—?' began Jake in a whisper.

At that moment the woman stepped closer - her face suddenly filling the screen.

Sid jumped up in panic and grabbed hold of my right arm. *'Get off!'* I murmured between clenched teeth, shaking myself free. Just then a beautiful voice filled the air all around.

'Charlie and Jake, thank you for coming to help Xong! And, Sid, thank you for your hospitality! Norman is back asleep. Do not worry.'

'Hospitality?!' muttered Jake under his breath.

'Xong?' I said, raising my eyebrows.

Sid stared at the lady dumbstruck and said nothing.

'Xong!' the beautiful lady repeated, smiling

again. 'You have no idea, Charlie, what trouble your Earth sport of football has caused my family!'

'Er...I'm very sorry,' I faltered. 'But there's no Xong here. We only have an Eeek. And our Eeek's got green skin and purple eyes. I really don't think he'd fit in with your family somehow.'

'But your Eeek *is* our Xong, Charlie!' the lady said, laughing. 'And *I* am Xong's mother!' Now I was really confused. So, I could see, were Sid and Jolio.

This didn't last long, because next thing the beautiful lady and man on Sid's telly began to go fuzzy at the edges - kind of like they were melting. Then, right before our eyes, they metamorphosed into two familiar green aliens, complete with semicircular ears, wafting blue smoke, and blinking plum-coloured eyes.

They remained this way for no more than a few seconds before slowly changing back into their human form.

'It's Eeek's parents from his photo!' whispered Jake.

'Cool,' murmured Sid. I could see he was already composing his next piece for Sci-Fi Weekly.

Just then a bright green light caught the corner of my eye. I glanced down to see Eeek's foot briefly poke out from under the bed. This wasn't the wisest of moves because next thing the dad alien's voice boomed angrily around the room making us all jump.

'Xong! Come out now please. It is time to go!'

'Please don't tell Eeek off!' I blurted out. 'He was going to come home after the party, really - *except Sid here kidnapped him!'*

I shot Sid a dark glance, but then immediately put my hand to my mouth in panic. What if the aliens *zapped* Sid there and then? Don't get me wrong, Sid's no great friend, but in the overall scheme of things, in that split second, I realised he probably did deserve to live.

Me and my big mouth!

'*Kidnapped?*' said Eeek's mum, in a quizzical echo. She tilted her head sideways as if she didn't understand.

'He's a fat liar! I no way kidnapped him!' cut in Sid. '*Charlie* kidnapped him. He was keeping him prisoner in his bedroom!'

'*What?*' I said indignantly. Now Sid was trying to get me zapped. 'That's rubbish! You're the kidnapper around here, Spiker! *And* you've been getting Eeek hyper on Red Bull. *And* your creepy brother stole money from my dad and sold him a tick—'

Eeek's mum's voice cut across my words and echoed around the room louder than ever.

'But Charlie, Sid didn't kidnap Xong!'

That shut me up, I have to admit. I furrowed my sticky brow in puzzlement. Sid folded his arms triumphantly and put on a self-satisfied grin.

Eeek's mum smiled out at us all.

'You see, boys,' she said, 'Xong invited herself to Sid's house to try to get tickets for the World Cup Final through his brother, Norman.'

I swear you could **see** the silence fill the room.

I glanced at Jake and Sid wondering if I'd misheard, but since their eyes were practically the size of dinner plates I knew I hadn't.

'**She?**' I said in a high voice after an awkward pause. I glanced back towards the bed where I could see a very faint glow of green.

'Eeek - *a girl?*' spluttered Jake, trying to contain his amusement. Sid just stared at the carpet.

Suddenly my cheeks began to burn: ***Eeek had seen me in my underpants at least ten times!***

'Of course!' said Eeek's mum laughing. 'Xong's very clever, you know. She will hold very high office one day! I just hope now we've let her visit you she will concentrate on her studies!'

'You mean you *knew* Eeek was going to run away?' I said weakly. Suddenly I felt doubly stupid.

'Of course!' said her mother. 'But we also knew she'd be safe in your hands. You see, Charlie, Xong did her Earth study on you. She knows everything about you there is to know!' By now my cheeks were volcanic.

Eeek's mum continued. 'She is desperate to impress you – and she loves your Earth sport of football!'

I was speechless and flattered. I stole a sideways glance at Sid who was still frowning at the carpet. To be honest I kind of felt sorry for him. I think he was feeling a bit used.

Xong's mother sighed. 'It is time for us to take her home now. I'm sorry for the trouble she has caused your father, Charlie. Norman tricked her with his ticket scam and she will learn from this. So will Norman - the police will be coming to see him tomorrow to give him a warning and he will return the money.'

Sid shuffled his feet awkwardly. What could he say?

'And now,' Eeek's mum went on, 'we really must be on our way. We need to transport Xong back to our spaceship.'

'Can we say goodbye?' I blurted out. I turned towards the bed where the glow of light was suddenly much stronger. Okay, so Eeek *was* a girl. So what? We'd been through so much together in the past two weeks and there was no way I just wanted her zapped away.

Jake started sniggering. 'Why, Charlie! You're not *in love* are you?'

Eeek's parents smiled politely as I shook my head and fought to hold back my tears.

Burning with embarrassment, I suddenly wondered if Jake could be right. Could yours truly, Charlie Spruit, aged only 11 and three quarters, be in love - with an *alien girl?* Or had I simply made a good friend who just so happened *not* to be a boy for once?

'Of course,' said Xong's mother smiling. 'Of course you can say goodbye. But we are nearly out of time.'

Eeek - or Xong, rather - was already crawling out from under the bed backwards. And when finally she stood up she gave us all an ear-touching alien grin.

'I'm sorry you have to go, Eeek!' I said faltering.

Eeek stepped forward and took my hand.

Her skin felt cool and firm, just like the time I'd brushed against it before. Jets of blue smoke began spurting from her ears, as if she was trying to say something.

Eeek's mum spoke again. 'Xong cannot transform to human likeness by herself yet, Charlie. But she is telling you she had a wonderful time.'

Eeek was now nodding vigorously, which made me smile.

'I'm sorry, but we really must go now as our energy is fading. We will transport you and Jake back home now. Do not worry about Sid and Norman. They will remember nothing about Xong once we've gone.'

Sid looked more than a little put out at this. I couldn't blame him really - I mean, imagine being *told* you won't remember that an alien spent the evening with you when all your life you've been a sci-fi fanatic.

I turned back to look at Eeek just as a jolt surged through my body and everything went dark.

Nineteen

My bottom hit a firm surface with a sharp thud and I opened my eyes to find myself sitting back on the floor in my bedroom next to Jake.

'Awesome!' he whispered looking all around wide-eyed.

'Look at that!' I cried jumping up. We dived towards the window.

An enormous purple disc hovered silently above

Sid's roofline. So strong was the glow, it lit up the whole of Sid Spiker's garden where Nipper stood dancing around on his hind legs wagging his tail!

I grabbed my telescope for a better look. At that moment Sid threw back his curtains. Seeing his look of panicked joy as he stared up at the spaceship I felt kind of both happy and sad for him because I knew he wouldn't remember any of it tomorrow.

I panned right towards the spaceship where a diagonal column of white light was suddenly beaming down in the direction of Sid's room, like it was providing a path up. But it was gone almost as soon as it had appeared.

The spaceship hovered for a few seconds more then streaked in a brilliant silent flash up towards the stars, leaving only the darkness and the moon behind.

I put down my telescope and looked out into the night sky. My stomach felt hollow. 'They've gone,' I said, my voice cracking.

Jake shrugged his shoulders and sighed.

'We are on our way, Charlie!' A girl's voice filled the room.

'What th—'.

We spun round.

Jake was ahead of me. He dived onto my bed where Eeek's little TV, which we'd left there earlier and forgotten about, lay glowing.

He grabbed it and passed it over. And now, with

Jake at my side, I saw Eeek, or Xong rather, in her human form smiling out at me.

I couldn't say anything at first, just kept swallowing hard and staring at her in disbelief. Just like the day we first met - except, of course, this time she was the human being and *I* was the bright green alien!

'Hi, Charlie! Hi Jake!' Xong was suddenly waving.

I pressed the zoom button so I could see her properly before she disappeared.

Xong, my alien girlfriend, actually looked really cool! She had short dark hair with a tiny fringe, smiling brown eyes and lots of fun freckles.

'I *love* your alien outfits!' she shouted.

I cleared my throat, but the words stuck fast.

'Sorry for all the trouble, Charlie!' She put her hand to her mouth and giggled again. 'I just didn't want to leave!'

'No trouble at all!' I replied bravely.

Can you believe it - my eyes were *brimming!*

'I'll miss you!' she called.

'It's time to go, Xong,' said her mother.

'Don't forget me, Charlie!'

'Of course not! Of course not!'

'Goodbye then, Charlie. Remember - **England for the Cup**! '

'England for the Cup!' I bellowed.

Xong stuck both thumbs up and grinned.

'*Eeeeeeek!*' she shouted one last time. Then, with a high-pitched whistle, the screen went blank and my alien girlfriend – and her little TV screen - disappeared.

For several minutes Jake and I sat on the bed in silence. I was grateful to Jake for this. I guess that's what best friends are for. Finally he cleared his throat and yawned. 'I'm off to sleep now,' he said with a sigh. 'Pretty weird she was a girl, eh?'

Jake clambered onto the Z-bed, still fused inside his alien suit. Two minutes later he was snoring just like my granddad.

As for me, well I just wasn't tired. I walked to my window and peered out. The sky was lit with a hundred thousand twinkling stars. Gazing up, I knew that somewhere out there was my Xong.

I picked a star, closed my eyes and wished that one day she might return. And as I turned and walked across to my bed I just hoped that she had heard.

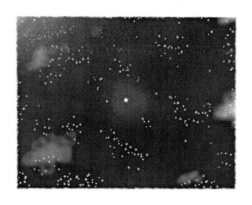

Eeeeek!

Also by Karen Inglis

The Secret Lake (8-11 yrs)
When Stella and her younger brother, Tom, move to their new London home they become mystified by the disappearances of Harry, their elderly neighbour's small dog. Where does he go? And why does he keep re-appearing wet-through?

Their quest to solve the riddle over the summer holidays leads to a boat buried under a grassy mound – and a tunnel that takes them to a secret lake. Soon they discover that they have travelled back in time to their home and its gardens 100 years earlier where they meet the children living there... As the story unfolds they make both friends and enemies, and uncover some startling connections between the past and present.

Search online or visit **thesecretlake.com**

Henry Haynes and the Great Zoo Escape (7-9 yrs) Just as Henry complains that his library book is boring, a huge hole appears on the page and sucks him down inside. Moments later he finds himself eyeball to eyeball with Brian, a very bossy boa constrictor who has his own plans for Henry... Visit **wellsaidpress.com** to find out more about the release date.

The Adventures of Ferdinand Fox (3-6 yrs)
Six delightful rhyming stories about Ferdinand the urban fox – a do-gooder and unsung hero. Read aloud or alone. Visit **ferdinandfox.co.uk** to find out more.

Had fun reading Eeek?
Please write a review!

Why not leave a review on Eeek's alien website - or ask the author a question?

Just go to **eeekthealien.com** and get writing!

(Karen usually replies within a day or two!)

And if you'd like to leave a review on your preferred online bookstore's website it will help other children find out about Eeek! (Ask a grown-up to help you.)

Top tip: be sure not to give away any alien secrets!

You can 'Like' Eeek at
facebook.com/eeekthealien

Follow Eeek on Twitter
@eeekthealien

Acknowledgments

With thanks once again to my good friend
Bridget Rendell for encouraging me to go the
extra mile with my alien tale, and for suggesting
useful edits along the way. To my mother for her
eagle-eye proofreading. To George and Nick for
inspiring the story and to Bob, George and Nick
for reading and offering invaluable consultancy
on the finer points of football etiquette!
Finally, to my illustrator, Damir, for his brilliance
and hard work.

About the author

Karen Inglis lives in Barnes, south-west London, England. She has two boys, George and Nick, who inspired her to write when they were younger. She also writes for business, but has more fun making up stories!

You can read more about Karen on her book websites **eeekthealien.com** and **thesecretlake.com** and **ferdinandfox.co.uk**

The Secret Lake ~ 5-Star reviews

"...an excellent read...because of the strong mix of characters it succeeds in being a book that can be appreciated by both boys and girls alike...(its) short, gripping chapters lead you swiftly on through an absorbing tale of mystery and suspense."

Louise Jordan, founder, The Writers' Advice Centre for Children's Books, London UK

Search online or visit The Secret Lake website to see what the children have to say!

www.thesecretlake.com

Order from your local bookshop or buy online.

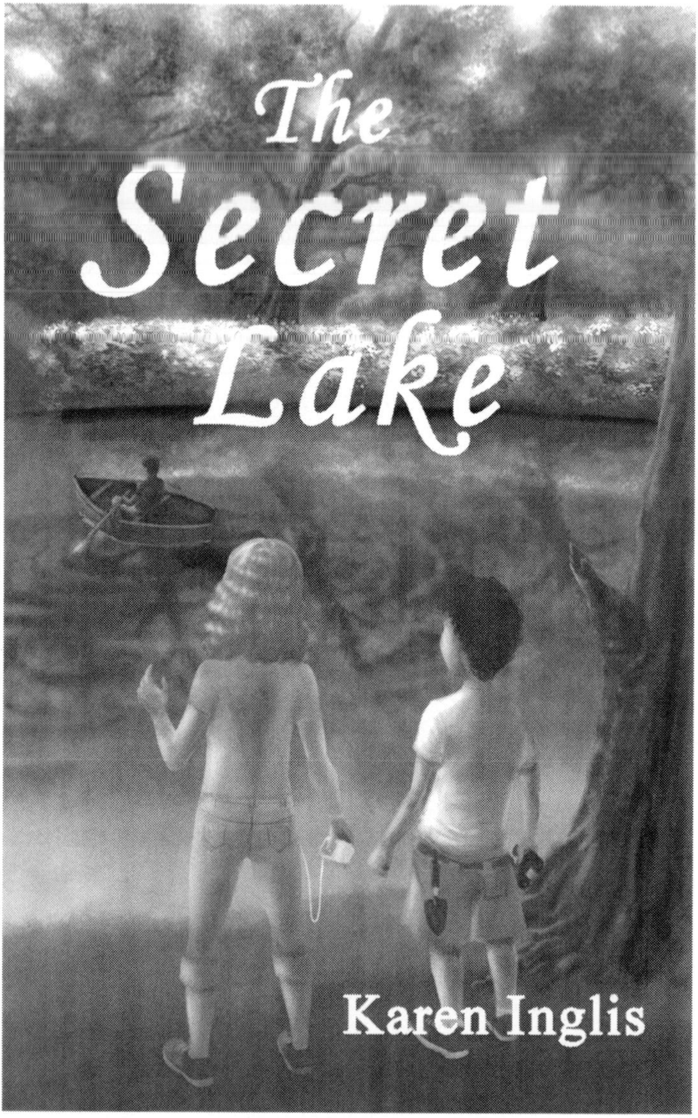
The Secret Lake
Karen Inglis

Lightning Source UK Ltd.
Milton Keynes UK
UKOW04f2153070316

269774UK00001B/1/P